MW00965637

Syndicate 6ix:

Flight of the Bluejay

Eric Raymond

Syndicate 6ix: Flight of the Bluejay

Copyright © 2018 Eric Raymond

All rights reserved

ISBN: 978-1-7323553-1-6 --- 978-1-7323553-2-3 (pbk.)

Published by: Eric Raymond 2018

Montgomery, Alabama

Syndicate 6ix and all titles, characters, their distinctive likeness, and related indicia are copyrights of Eric Raymond © 2018. The characters, names, and incidents mentioned in this publication are fictitious and any resemblance to real persons, living or dead, is purely coincidental.

No parts of this book may be reproduced in any form or by any electronic, mechanical, photocopying, recording, or otherwise, without the prior written permission of the copyright owner.

Editor: Allison Adams

Cover Photography by Ariel Cox, @ladybehindthelens_

Thank-you to Bobby, Ariel, and Kayla for constantly inspiring me to keep moving forward, thank-you to Tyler and Kylie for your support, and special thanks to my parents and grandparents for always believing in me.

Flight of the Bluejay

Flight of the Bluejay Part One:

He stood perched atop the clocktower with the wind to his back while he scouted the city down below. Sirens wailed in the distance and the stench from Pongoli's Pizza Place wafted from around the corner mercifully extinguishing the smell of piss from the back alley nearby.

Ember City was one of the largest cities in the nation, and the old money upon which it was built still pumps through its veins. The police and government officials were mostly corrupt, and crime was so commonplace that it's a wonder any sane person would choose to live there, but cost of living was low, and, beyond the crime, the city was full of opportunities for the common man to find his place in the world. Only problem was, the common man had to survive long enough to do so and that was much easier said than done.

However, the city had its protectors: Aves and his sidekicks, Yellow Bittern and Bluejay, spent their days combating Ember City's darkness in hopes that one day the light would shine through.

It was his first solo mission in years, and though he appeared calm from his vantage point, his nerves had never been more on edge. Declan Parks, Bluejay, was patrolling the city hoping to take down one of its most notorious criminals, Mr. E, the chemist for the Nova Organization for Viable Analysis Corporation.

N.O.V.A. was an underground operation with its hand in many pots, but they were mostly known for creating and distributing a drug known as NV-15 which gave normal, everyday humans the temporary ability to be extraordinary. The drug did this by manipulating the Nova gene and was highly addictive and extremely dangerous. If Declan could take Mr. E. down, he would bring down N.O.V.A.'s entire infrastructure and bringing them down was his top priority. He had firsthand knowledge of how destructive NV-15 could be, and he would stop at nothing to cleanse his city of the drug. He had once fallen victim to NV-15's promise; the promise of power was too good to pass up.

Having spent his early years in the shadow of his parents, and his later years in the shadow of his mentor, Aves, Declan would have given anything to be more than he was. His mother, Beacon, had the ability to absorb solar energy and convert it into immeasurable physical strength and speed. His father, Zipline, could move at supersonic speeds and vibrate through solid objects. He looked up to his parents; he wanted to be like them and join their side in the superhero team known as Right Eye, but his powers never developed. It was like a slap in the face that he was extraordinarily, helplessly normal. It was an unmistakable grievance, one that would drive a wedge between him and his parents up until their dying day.

After his parent's death, Declan was taken in by Hank Alverez who fought alongside Declan's parents in Right Eye as the vigilante codenamed Aves. Declan had always admired Hank for doing what his parents did but without the bonus of superpowers. Hank was a skilled martial artist, acrobat, and gymnast; he had a genius level IQ, advanced knowledge of technologies, and his bulletproof suit equipped with hi-tech weaponry and defense systems allowed him to fly and granted him limited invisibility. He did not let his shortcomings stop him from fighting right alongside his more powerful allies, and he taught Declan that his dreams of being a hero were not limited to having superpowers. The two trained together night and day, and before long, Declan became "Bluejay" and took to protecting the streets under Aves' wings.

For years, the two fought crime together; they became the beacon of hope that was noticeably missing in the darkness of the city. However, when a drug came along that could right the gratuitous wrong that was Declan's life, he could not let the opportunity pass without at least testing the waters. Hank had taught him being a hero was more than just superpowers, but Declan still always wondered "what if?"

It started off as an experiment, but it wasn't long before it spiraled into a full-blown addiction. While on NV-15, he had the power of telepathy, his senses were enhanced, he could generate illusions, and cast thoughts. It made him feel like a new man, it made him feel invincible. Never mind that the drug made him feel volatile and warped his mind, he was unstoppable, and any criminal who opposed him risked having their mind shattered.

Hank saw his protégé slipping further and further into the darkness but no matter how much Hank tried to help, Declan kept pulling away. After seemingly endless bickering the two of them eventually parted ways and Declan took up the new codename "Vigil."

He used his NV-15 induced powers to clean up the streets of Ember City in a way that Aves and Bluejay never could: no more hiding in the shadows and no more holding back. Vigil was judge, jury, and if he deemed it necessary, executioner. As he slipped deeper and deeper into addiction he became less aware of his own actions; one pill every few hours soon turned to four or five just to stay afloat. His skin became stretched tight over his bones, and his eyes became sunken in from the heavy abuse, but the power coursing through his veins was a worthwhile tradeoff. That is, until July seventeenth, a date that would stick in his mind forever.

As Vigil, Declan was following a lead on a sex-trafficking ring headed by the criminal mastermind known as Lavender Madame. She had been a ghost for so long, but Declan managed to track down one of the girls that used to work for Madame, and it was his mission to get as much intel out of her as possible.

The girl's name was Sarah Hara. She was a young Latina who got bored of her life in the suburbs and decided to run away to the city, but she was unprepared for such a life, and the city ended up swallowing her whole. Eventually, she managed to escape Madame's clutches and piece some semblance of a life back together. She found a place just outside of Ember City in a tiny studio apartment above a noisy nightclub, far removed from the upper-middle class suburb home she had run away from only a few years ago.

That night she had just gotten home from a busy shift at a nearby diner and wanted nothing more than to grab the closest bottle of wine and sink into a lavender scented bath, but her plans were interrupted when she noticed a shadowy figure standing just beyond the moonlight's fingertips. Without hesitation, she pulled a G26 Glock from her purse and aimed it unwaveringly in the shadow's direction.

"Who are you?" Her voice was mixed with aggression and hesitation.

Declan stepped from the shadows with his hands raised. Normally, any woman who gazed upon his thick muscles, tan skin, and hazel eyes would swoon and let their guard down, but he was a mere skeleton of his former self and the sick looking man before her put her even more on edge. She released the safety.

"My name is Vigil," he smiled but it was not as charming as he intended.

"And?"

"I have some questions about Lavender Madame, and I was hoping you could answer them. It's time for her operation to fold and you may be the final nail in her coffin."

She stood quiet for a moment before letting out a boisterous laugh, "Are you out of your mind? I'm not helping you! I barely escaped that place with my life! If I open my mouth I will be snatched up in the blink of an eye."

"There are hundreds of other girls and guys just like you, and you can help save them." He had expected her answer and was ready with a rebuttal.

"And risk my own safety?" Her aim became steadier, "I don't think so."

"How can you be so selfish?" He prepared himself. The look in her eyes told him everything he needed to know.

She sighed, "When you've lived my life you have the right to be."

He knew what he had to do, and his face looked forlorn like a small voice was telling him it was not too late to turn back, but the voice was too small.

"You've made your choice then." The room grew eerily quiet and his eyes went white. Her hair flew back as if an imaginary gust of wind blew through the apartment as Declan reached out to her with his mind.

She involuntarily lowered her weapon and closed her eyes while inhaling sharply. This feeling was familiar: the feeling of someone else's mind entering her psyche; a stranger in her own head trying to sift through private moments and trudging up old memories that were meant to be cast aside. It was a feeling she knew all too well, and a feeling she had trained herself against. She pushed back and cast Declan out of her head. The force of the mental push almost toppled him backwards out of the open window, but he managed to brace himself at the last second. For only a moment he hesitated; a moment was all Sarah needed. She lifted her Glock and opened fire on him.

The first bullet whizzed by his ear leaving an irritating humming in its wake. Declan ducked to the ground, rolled to the other side of the room, sprang to his feet, and barely got grazed by the third or fourth shot. He focused his mind and reached out to Sarah again. He was unprepared for resistance last time, but this time he knew he needed a little extra push. He found her mind again and it felt like a heavily guarded fortress. It was cloudy like he was trudging through a swamp filled with quicksand, but she could not keep him out forever.

"You don't think Lavender Madame trained us against mind tricks," She winced as she fought back against his intrusion. The Glock was by her waist as she settled her mind. "All those creeps. You don't think one or two of them were legit Novas?"

"*I'm sorry you had to live that life, and I'm sorry I'm making you relive it, but I need answers. Yours is not the only life worth saving.*" She heard the voice clear as day but saw his lips were not moving.

He was inside her; he had penetrated her barriers. Thinking about her time with Lavender

Madame while she gloated was all it took for him to find a crack in her fortress and slip in.

She would not let him take her thoughts. She saw the memories as he traveled through them, and that was not a road she wanted to go back down. The past was the past and it was going to stay that way. She pushed back once more but his mind had its claws in hers. She pushed back harder and felt his grip lessen so she pushed back even harder.

"Don't do this. Just let me get what I need and leave. If you resist…" The rest of his words were cut off as a bullet pierced his side.

Momentarily, she quit resisting and seized the opportunity to shoot him. Her mind was groggy, so her aim was a little off, but the wound was enough for Vigil to relinquish his hold. He stumbled back and braced himself on a half-put-together dresser as blood began to pour out of the hole in his shirt.

"Son of a…"

He found her eyes; she tried to turn and run, but it was already too late. With a furious intensity he jumped to her mind. Her head flew back at the sheer force of the psychic wave and her feet lifted from the ground and sent Sara toppling onto her back.

Vigil stalked over to her as he clawed his way through her mind with abandoned fervor. He shredded through her past inch by inch in an enraged state as the blood from his side fueled his rage. He tore through her mind until he found what he was looking for, Lavender Madame's base of operations.

He relaxed his mind and eased out of hers, his pupils swam back to hazel, his breathing became easy, and he wiped a trickle of blood from his nose. He looked down and found Sarah on the ground. "I'm sorry I had to do that," he said before propping her up. Her body was limp in his arms and a trail of drool escaped her mouth. His eyes went wide when they found hers; her pupils were enlarged but void of emotion.

He propped her against the wall and jumped to his feet in a panic. "I can fix this."

He nervously brushed his hand through his wavy hair and tried to come up with a plan, "I can fix this."

He repeated the phrase to himself as if the answer would reveal itself if he had enough faith. "I can fix this."

He looked back to her, her eyes were still wide and her mouth still open and leaking as her body began to twitch slightly. Declan gritted his teeth, "I just need to put her back together!" He fumbled in his cloak pockets and withdrew three small pills, "I just need to be stronger and I can put her back together."

He downed the pills and waited anxiously. He grew impatient after a minute and withdrew a few more pills from his pocket and threw those back as well. Another minute passed, and his body began to tingle as power surged through him. "I can do this." He turned back towards her and placed a hand on her forehead.

The power coursing through him was intense and warmed him entirely. It was like he was bathing in a hot spring. He could see in her mind as clearly as he could see his own and he swiftly tried to correct his mistakes, but as he went on he could feel the power fading. He popped a few more pills and continued his work. He simply kept swallowing them, one after the other. The warmness in his body grew less and less pleasant and began to burn and itch just beneath the surface of his skin. He continued trying to piece her mind back together, but he could not focus once his heart began to race and his own mind began to fade with each heartbeat growing louder and louder in his ears.

He fell back and gasped while fighting for each breath he took as his lungs felt like they were on fire. His eyes rolled back into his head, his body began to convulse, and the next thing he knew there was nothing.

Darkness.

Emptiness.

The world around him grew cold as he let out his dying breath, but he was okay with dying. He did not know how he could face himself after destroying Sarah's mind, and now he didn't have to. Yes, it was a cowardly thought, but he went peacefully as the darkness washed over him.

****

He woke up a few days later back in the BirdCage with Hank sitting at his bedside. Hank wore a worried look that only parents get after their children do something absurdly stupid. They did not talk about it much, but Declan could always feel Hank looking over his shoulder afraid that anything and everything was going to send him back down the NV-15 path, and it took months of convincing before Hank let Declan take up the mantle of Bluejay again. It was not like it was before; that bond of trust between them was sullied beyond repair, but they worked well together, that was undeniable.

A few years had passed since the incident with Sara Harah; tonight was the first night Declan had been out on his own. He peered over the side of the clocktower and noticed his mark had just entered the alley across the street between the library and the bike shop. The man in a grey sweatshirt was a low-level dealer but he was set to meet with his supplier. NV-15 had been replaced by a more aggressive version known as NV-17, and it was Declan's job to take down the supplier which would hopefully lead him back to Mr. E.

After a few minutes, the man in the hoodie exited the alley with a duffle-bag and took a left towards the bike shop.

"Dealer's headed your way, Yellow."

A voice answered its acknowledgement through his earpiece, and at the same time, a petite looking figure in a black hoodie exited the alley and took a right towards the library. Declan climbed down the face of the clocktower using his talon-like gauntlets and landed across the street directly in front of his mark.

"This can go one of two ways," he said confidently.

His mark smirked from underneath his hoodie, "I was wondering when I'd run into you."

They threw off their hoodie revealing a bright, scarlet leather jacket and matching leather pants and boots. Her pale skin almost matched the color of her bleach blonde hair that was pulled tight into a ponytail with not a single hair out of place. She wore a crazed look through interesting makeup as she met his eyes, "Long time no see."

Declan was motionless as he stared at the unmistakable form of Sarah Hara.

Part Two: Relapse of the Bluejay

She was right there standing in front of him, a ghost from his past, the biggest mistake in his life… Sarah Hara. She was far from the vegetative state he had left her in, and there was no denying she was not the same innocent girl on the run from Lavender Madame. She was surer of herself than before, and he couldn't help but feel that was not a good thing for him.

"S-Sarah?"

He knew it was her, but everything inside of him wished it wasn't.

A thin smile curled the sides of her lips, "Not quite." She retrieved a crowbar from her back and lunged forward without another word. She swung wildly with a crazed look of determination on her face.

Declan jumped to the side narrowly missing the first swipe, and when her hand came back around he caught her by the wrist, folded her arm behind her, and held her back to his chest. A loud clank sounded as the crowbar hit the ground and Sarah winced.

"I don't want to hurt you, Sarah."

She cackled making an offputtingly hideous sound, "That sounds familiar."

She threw her head back, and the distinct sound of crushing cartilage rang out as Bluejay released his grasp and clenched his nose which started to flow with crimson tide.

"I'm going to enjoy this."

She picked up her crowbar from the sidewalk and flew towards him once more.

He dodged left then right, expertly missing each one of her attacks, but he refused to fight back. The more he evaded her the more pissed off she seemed to become. There was an anger in her eyes; one that could only be quenched by blood. His blood. He tried to figure out a plan to take her down without harming her, but every conclusion he came to ended with Sara getting hurt in some type of way. He knew he only had one choice; it was a gamble, but it was his best option to resolve things peacefully.

He did a backflip to give himself some distance; then he stood in front of her with his arms to his sides. She narrowed her eyebrows and let out a scream as she rushed towards him. He did not flinch, and as she closed the distance between them the wind seemed to blow right out of her sails. She made it to him, the crowbar still raised, but she did not bring it down.

"What's the deal?" She said with a nasty attitude as she brought the crowbar nonchalantly to her side, "How can I get my revenge if you don't fight back?"

"I don't want to hurt you, Sarah, I mean that."

"QUIT calling me Sarah! She huffed, "Sarah is dead."

An uncomfortable silence lingered for a moment before she caught his eye, "You know that better than anyone. My name is Scarlet Harlot. Now," she whipped the crowbar back into his face and took a fighting stance, "fight me."

"What happened to you?" His voice broke as he stared at her. Thoughts of that night came flooding back to him, and he took a step back as if he was preparing to physically run away from his past.

She paused for a moment looking him over with a curious expression before a smile broke through her lips and a hoarse cackle jumped from her throat, "Birdman didn't tell you!?"

She doubled over with laughter as Declan peered at her. "That night after you collapsed, Aves found us. I watched, trapped inside my own mind unable to move or speak as he tried saving you. After his failed attempts, he finally picked you up and carried you to the window. He looked back at me. I could tell he knew I wasn't dead, but you were more important, so he left me there, sitting in my own drool, as he leapt from the building whisking you away to safety. Apparently, wherever he took you did the job cause here you are.

"My journey? Not so peaceful. After what felt like days, sitting in my own filth my unexpected hero finally arrived in the form of Violet Strumpet, one of Lavender Madame's girls. She took me back to their base, and Madame had one of her clients piece me back together. Even with my mind whole, I was still weak and fractured, so I took a page out of your book and turned to good ole NV. Turns out, I don't have the nova gene, so beyond this cosmetic shift," she pointed to her pale skin and matching hair, "I didn't get anything but the world's best high.

"Anyway, an addict with no job eventually has to do some things she's not proud of. One thing led to another, and here I am paying off a debt with Lavender Madame by working for Mr. E. I'm surprised Birdbrain didn't tell you though," she chuckled, "we've had quite a few run ins."

Declan was silent for an uncomfortable length of time while he tried to find the right words to somehow make things better, but when no remedy came, he chose to say, "Sarah, I'm sorry. I never meant for any of this to happen."

"No problem," she smiled, "Mine was not the only life worth saving."

Her face fell to a scowl as his words from the past left her lips in the present. "How did saving all those other kids go for you?" She cackled again and brought the crowbar down hard on his face, her laugh growing increasingly more unhinged with each swing.

"Enough!" Aves jumped from a nearby rooftop and landed just behind Scarlet.

Scarlet brought the crowbar up once more, but her arm was caught by a grappling line, and she was pulled back. Aves caught her and handcuffed her to a streetlight pole in one swift motion. She growled like a deranged animal after him as he walked by her and he crouched near Declan who was still lying on the ground.

"Bluejay, are you okay?" Aves voice was deep and strong.

Declan pushed Aves away and picked himself up off the cold concrete. His hair was matted with blood and one of his eyes was swollen closed. He wiped a trickle of blood from his busted lip and began to walk away without a word.

"Meet me back at the BirdCage. We need to talk." Aves voice was stern but sincere as he turned to walk away; he stopped and glanced back at Declan.

After a moment, Declan turned around to respond, but Hank had already disappeared into the night. He sighed heavily, and his eyes struck something familiar on the ground. Something familiar, yet he could tell a distinct difference; like an old friend he hadn't seen in a while reemerging with a noticeable weight loss or faux hair.

NV-17, a lone pill in a small baggie. It must have slipped from the case when Scarlet Harlot and her associate made the drop. He nudged it with his boot for a moment then looked over towards Scarlet.

She wore a sinister grin on her face as if Declan's finding of the pill had been her plan along. She never wanted to take him down; she wanted him to face his own demons. She wanted him to sweat, and right now he was drowning. She watched him closely while he went back and forth with the struggle in his mind.

Eventually, he picked it up and rolled it around in his palm. He noticed Scarlet perk up like she had just won the lottery.

"Settle down," he said impatiently, "Aves will want to analyze this. We're getting close to bringing this operation down."

"So, you think," her grin unwavering with a secret just behind her chapped lips.

"The cops will be by in a second, try not to go anywhere." He frowned for a moment at what she had become because of him; then he grappled onto the rooftops and made his way to one of the secluded entrances of his hideout.

The BirdCage, Aves and Bluejay's base, was hidden away inside of a mountain just outside of Ember City, and there were many entrances sprinkled throughout the city for quick access to whatever crime was being undertaken on any given night.

Declan entered the abandon warehouse district, made his way to building 312, and slipped through the boarded-up door. He found his way to the back wall, felt along the brick until he found the right one with his index finger, and he held it there for a moment until a chime sounded.

"Welcome Master Bluejay," A disembodied voice sounded in the cluttered darkness. Gears and pistons began to whir and the brick in the wall began to separate from itself. The wall folded in on itself until an entryway was presented, and Declan entered the elevator. The wall's ends found each other again behind him leaving the abandoned building to its

lonely silence once more. He pressed the button labeled 'C' and the shaft began to move.

On his ride to the BirdCage, Declan removed his communication device, so he could mull over the night's events. A task hard to do when his teammate, Yellow Bittern, kept trying to buzz in every other minute.

He didn't know what he was going to say to Hank once he saw him. Hank knew the whole time that Sarah was alive and that she was running drugs for Mr. E. and Lavender Madame; he knew and, yet he never decided to mention it. Declan knew that if he brought it up Hank would just play it off as trying to protect Declan's feelings, but that was unacceptable. The night Sarah died almost destroyed Declan, and if there was anyway she survived he would have wanted to know. It was unfair for Hank to keep that from him, and he needed to answer for it.

The ride came to a halt outside of the entrance, and Declan made his way off the elevator and into the BirdCage. Hank was sitting in his office chair with his cowl by his side and a long expression on his face. Declan rarely noticed how old his mentor had gotten, but in that moment the years on him were apparent.

"Declan…"

"You had no right," His voice was uneasy as his emotion seemed to grip him by the throat.

Hank stood up and walked over to Declan and grabbed him by the shoulders, "Declan," he said again.

Declan slapped Hanks hands away, "You had no right!" He threw his fist into the air and it came to an almost instant stop as it landed with a crash against Hank's cheek.

Hank took two steps back and looked at the man standing before him. He had taken Declan in at such a young age and had molded him from a scared young orphan into a crimefighting hero. In that moment, he couldn't help but look on him as a mistake. It was a mistake to take him in, it was a mistake to train him, and it was a mistake to trust him. He had done nothing but disappoint him. As much as he wanted to think differently he couldn't help but feel regret as he looked at his protégé. "I don't owe you anything."

"Excuse me!?" Declan planted his feet as a fire ran up his spine.

"I've raised you from a boy and taught you everything you need to know about this life, and I've given you ample opportunity to succeed but you insist on failing. I didn't tell you because I didn't have to. I am the leader, you are the sidekick. If you would have known she was out there you would have gone out of your way to do something dumb." The words hung in the air like an unwelcomed guest loitering in the awkward silence that followed. "I'm sorry, Declan, but I did what was right."

"No. You did what was right for *you*. You saw how bad I was struggling and the one bit of information that could have saved me you decided to keep to yourself, and you didn't even help her! You left her there that night, and when you saw her running around with Mr. E. and Lavender Madame you still did nothing! You're no hero." Declan tried and failed to hold back the rage that was building inside of him. "You never forgave me for that night. You never will forgive me for that night. Go ahead and say it!"

Hank scoffed, "Of course I won't! I took you in! I raised you like a son and gave you a good home, and you throw it all away over some drug? Just so you can feel powerful?" He slammed his fist on the table.

"There was more to it than that," he said weakly while he shifted uncomfortably.

"Then tell me what. Tell me what was so important that you had to stay doped up. Tell me what was so important that you had to risk your life every single day?"

For a moment Declan considered answering him truthfully. He considered telling him that having powers made him feel close to his parents in some sick and twisted way, but all that came out was, "I don't owe you anything."

Hank's face fell in disbelief and Declan could almost see Hank's heart break, "Get out," he said mournfully.

"Gladly." Declan turned around and began to make his way back to the elevator when a siren sounded, and red lights began to swim around the cave. Just then a face wearing a black and yellow mask popped up on the large monitor in the center of the cave

"Why the hell aren't you two picking up your communicators!?" Yellow Bittern sounded winded and the sound of a motorcycle roared off screen while her heir was flying all around her.

"We're kind of busy Darcy." Hank turned from Declan and walked over to the screen.

"Well things are about to get a lot busier," she said with a tone. She hated when Hank tried to dismiss her.

"What's going on?"

"I don't know how they found it, but Mr. E. and Lavender Madame are headed straight for you. I followed the dealer back to his place and after some interrogation he said something was going down at the Lavender Lounge. I headed that way, and that's when I spotted Mr. E., Madame, and a small group of N.O.V.A. soldiers piling into a helicopter. I've been following it, and we're on the outskirts of town now. There is only one thing out this way."

"The BirdCage. But how?"

"I think I know how…" Declan retrieved the NV-17 from his pocket and noticed the tiniest red speck blinking off and on at the bottom of the baggy. "They played us."

A wave of guilt came crashing over him; he could feel himself sinking under Hank's disappointed glare.

The light blinked steadily as Mr. E. and Lavender Madame drew ever nearer to the BirdCage.

Part 3: Fall of the Bluejay

Declan held up the plastic bag in despair as the weight of yet another mistake began to sink in.

"They played us." His tone was defeated, and his shoulders slumped.

"No," Hank stalked over to Declan and swiped the bag from his hand and examined it, "They played you."

"I-I only brought it to help, so we could analyze it and…"

Hank scoffed, "I'm not naïve, boy. You brought this back because you couldn't help yourself, and that's what they were counting on. NV-17 has been on the streets for months, and you don't think I've already analyzed a sample? Don't give me that weak excuse. You've put this whole operation in jeopardy!"

He threw the baggie hard at Declan's chest; it smacked him and fell limp to the floor.

"A.N.I.T.A. defensive maneuvers," Hank called out for the BirdCage's artificial intelligence system.

A silence creeped in, and Hank looked around and noticed Yellow Bittern was no longer on the computer screen. In fact, all the computer screens were black, and the intruder alarm had stopped ringing and the lights had turned back to their normal state.

"A.N.I.T.A.," Hank Questioned.

Before Hank could investigate the problem further his head jerked back as his body flew forward.

"You don't want to do this." He regained his composure and turned towards Declan.

Declan lifted his fist and lunged forward. Hank sidestepped and dodged the attack easily and used Declan's own momentum against him. His protégé went flailing passed him, and Hank landed a devastating elbow to Declan's back causing him to land face first on the floor.

Declan rolled over and sprung to his feet, "You never trusted me. Even before the NV you always saw me as a noose around your neck. You were never a team player!" he spat each word at Hank with venomous rage.

"Right Eye was my life, of course I'm a team player! I just need teammates that I can trust."

"Bullshit!" Declan lunged forward again and swung at Hank. The punch barely brushed his chin, but Hank didn't notice it was a feint until it was too late. The second punch landed squarely into his stomach, and he doubled over with a wheeze.

"You don't think I remember my parents talking about Aves? How many missions you put in jeopardy because you were always running off alone? Hell, it's probably because of you they died during the Blue Moon mission!"

"You… Little…" Hank threw his fist at him, but Declan quickly ducked out of the way and landed another body shot sending a pulse of pain throughout Hank's body.

Anger raged through Declan's eyes as he stood over his mentor, his father figure. He went in for another shot, but Hank pushed him off. Declan stumbled back, and Hank closed the distance between them landing three deafening blows as he went.

Declan went down again but managed to struggle his way back to his feet.

"Stay. Down." Hank pitied the boy and didn't know what he was trying to prove; all he wanted was for him to stop. It was true he and Declan had their differences, but Declan was still the boy he raised like his own. He was still the closest thing he would ever have to a child.

Declan moved forward again, and Hank threw a sluggish punch which Declan easily slipped under. The next thing Hank knew his bottom row of teeth were rising to meet the top row as Declan landed an uppercut. Hank hit the ground hard just as a ding chimed in the background and the elevator doors swung open.

Declan's eyes went wide when the occupants stepped into the BirdCage. The first was a peculiar looking man in half-moon glasses and a pristine white lab-coat. He was followed by an elegant woman with long black hair wearing a lavender hanfu.

"Don't speak," ordered Hank; he did not attempt to hide his contempt for Declan as he picked himself up off the floor while Mr. E., Lavender Madame, and their handful of soldiers made their way deeper into the BirdCage towards Aves and Bluejay.

That base was all Hank had. Even when Right Eye disbanded he still had the BirdCage to go back to; it was his home away from home, and now it was no longer safe. He would have to move his hideout to another location, and that was a travesty. A travesty he felt had brought on himself.

He had never wanted kids, but when his friends died in combat he considered it an honor to raise their child for them. He did not know at the time what he had gotten himself into. He loved Declan like his own, but the boy always made critical mistakes. Still, Hank trained him to become a leader, but despite that training, he feared Declan would never become one.

He sighed deeply.

Mr. E. chuckled softly as he took his glasses off and retrieved a cloth from his pocket.

"Aves," he said in an amused voice while he began scrubbing his lenses.

He lifted them to the light to see if they were without blemish and was pleased at their cleanliness. He put his glasses back on and the cloth back into his pocket and met Hank's eye with a sinister smile.

"Aves. In all my years I would have never guessed that the great Aves was none-other than washed up play-write Hank Angel Alvarez. Quite amusing don't you think, Missy?"

"Quite." Lavender Madame looked bored as she peered around the BirdCage. "Can we get what we came for? One of us has a business to run; My time is valuable."

"Yes, yes all right. Aves... Hank, can you please direct us to your server? We've already combed through your system thanks to my nifty friend," he pointed to the abandoned baggy with the tracking chip and NV-17 in it, "but we didn't find any of your notes or research on N.O.V.A. I must say, you've been quite the pest, but you've been manageable up until now. Unfortunately, you've gotten a little too close and your minor annoyance has caught the eye of some rather large associates." He shrugged nonchalantly.

"Anyway, smart man like you probably keeps that on a separate server just in case someone gets on the main system. If you would be so kind as to point us in the right direction?"

"I won't tell you anything," he said with conviction. He looked around the room trying to think of any tool he could use to gain the upper hand. All he needed was a little time.

"Pity; I had hoped you'd be more forthcoming, but as Missy stated, we really must be getting along, and we can find it with or without you now that we're here."

Mr. E. motioned with his index and pointer finger, waived one of the soldiers forward, and the soldier took aim at Hank.

It occurred so fast that Declan almost did not register what happened. The sound was deafening and absolute and a deep weight dropped to the pit of his stomach like his heart had given up.

"H-" before Declan could say his name another shot sounded, and Declan fell to the ground. He tried moving, but his limbs did not respond as he stared at Hank's lifeless body.

"Gracious!" Mr. E. removed a handkerchief and dabbed red spots from his lab-coat in disgust.

Lavender Madame rolled her eyes, "What did you think would happen when you shot them?"

"I knew it would be messy, but that doesn't mean I have to like it."

"Whatever," she looked around and noticed a small panel on the back wall. "If a server is going to be anywhere I bet it would be there. Kolt, be a doll and retrieve the data. A dead man can't tell tales, but I don't want any of his super-friends wandering in and getting any bright ideas. Clean his research now before it gets anymore eyes on it."

A short man with an athletic build came strutting to the front of the group. He removed his helmet and gloves and placed them on a nearby desk. His hazel eyes met Declan's briefly, but he looked away because he could not bear the sight. Kolt smoothed back his ginger hair, walked over to the keypad on the back wall and hooked up a small device to it. His shoulders were hunched as he worked because he could feel the weight of his bosses' eyes on him, but luckily the device screamed after only a few painful seconds, and a hidden door revealed itself behind the wall.

Kolt opened the door and entered the hidden office where a single server and monitor were hooked up. He plugged in a flash-drive and moved through a few screens while removing all the data from the server and copying it to his device.

"He was one of yours wasn't he," Mr. E. asked as they watched Kolt work.

Lavender Madame smiled, "Yes; brought in a lot of money. People always want an exotic, taboo experience. N.O.V.A. wanted him for other skills though, so who was I to deny them?" she shrugged.

She looked around once more at the monitors, training area, and breakfast nook, "I can see the appeal of this place. Maybe I'll have Kolt install some new security measures and take it for my own. Can never have too many hideouts, and this one *is* newly vacant."

Her lips curled into a devilish smile as she noticed Declan was still squirming around. "Poor little birdboy," she squatted next to him and tilted her head in a curious manor. "Still refusing to die," she poked her finger into the bullet wound in his gut and Declan cried out in pain. "All those years tracking me and now my new home will be on your grave." She stood over him, "Almost poetic don't you think?"

"It's unbecoming to play with your food," Mr. E. sighed. "Just finish him off."

"What's the fun in that? Letting him bleed out is much more exhilarating."

Mr. E. sighed again loudly to show his disdain for her as Kolt returned to the party. "Did you collect all of the data?"

"Yes sir," he said in a meek voice. He had a slight Asian accent he could not seem to shake even though he had been in America for most of his life. He handed a small stack of papers to Lavender Madame, "These were in there as well."

She scanned them over, "Thank-you, Kolt, we'll dispose of these. You've done well today." She noticed the grim look on his face, "Smile," she took his face in her hand softly, "Because of you, Aves and Bluejay have finally been brought down," She kissed him on the cheek. "N.O.V.A. will be pleased of your work. Come now, before the stench of death sets in."

She took Kolt arm and arm, and they followed Mr. E. and the soldiers back to the elevator to begin their descent down the mountain.

The silence that lingered was loud and heavy as Declan lie on the ground grasping for air; hoping that each breath was not his last. He stared straight up at the ceiling feeling his life fade with each passing second. He could feel Hank's cold eyes staring at him from the left, and he let out a whimper. The thought that it was all his fault slammed to the forefront of his mind; a tear rolled down his cheek, and his head slumped to the right. When he opened his eyes, he felt another inch closer to death, and part of him welcomed it. He lay still in the openness of the BirdCage waiting for time to reach its end, but then he noticed something laying next to him within his grasp, the baggie with the NV-17.

     He sluggishly moved his hand towards it, balled his fist around the baggie, and brought it up to his lips. He slowly ripped off the top of the baggie with his teeth and let the pill drop onto his tongue. He figured if he was going to die, he might as well get one last high. No one was around to be ashamed of him anymore. He felt the pill tingle his tongue and he closed his mouth and felt it slide to the back of his throat.

     Declan's whole body was warm like fire had risen inside him, but it did not burn. He embraced the warmth and closed his eyes as his senses faded into nothing. He was going to meet his maker and could feel his soul floating away when he heard a scream from the darkness.

"Declan!"

His eyes shot open and he realized it wasn't his soul that was flying. He was alive. He was alive and hovering over the ground. He turned around and spotted Yellow Bittern standing in the entryway with her eyes wide and her hand over her mouth in disbelief.

Bluejay found his wings.

Elle is next in line to become Mother Nature, the Goddess of Order, but that is the last thing she wants to do. She sets out on a journey to find her long lost sister, so her sister can take the throne and leave Elle to follow her dream of living her life on the surface world. What she hoped would be an easy task turns to chaos when she finds out the truth about her past.

Turn the page for a preview of what's to come in the next installment of <u>The Six</u>, "Order and Chaos."

Order and Chaos
Part One: Elle's Fire

"Ini'el."

A husky looking woman came storming through the open door of the tavern. It was mid-morning, so it was mostly empty except for a few stragglers drowning their sorrows. One of these loungers included a curly-haired beauty sitting alone at the bar lost in a goblet of wine.

Her shoulders slumped like they carried the weight of the world and her eyes told the story of a sadness she seemed much too young to know.

"What are you doing here?" The husky women asked.

"What does it look like I'm doing? I'm hiding out…and day-drinking," the girl took another swig from her goblet making it a point not to turn and greet the woman.

The husky woman placed her hands on her hips and furrowed her brow, "Young lady, your coronation is in two weeks' time. You need to be training, not drowning your brain!" She snatched the goblet from the girl's lips and slammed it on the counter.

The girl scoffed; her eyes started glowing a light blue shade, and the water in a nearby barrel began to dance back and forth; it picked itself up and dropped with a splash back into the container.

She blinked. Her eyes transitioned from blue to a burning orange, and flames leapt from the lantern on the wall and pranced around the air before returning to its holster. Another blink and her eyes became a brilliant green. She touched the dead plant at the edge of the bar, and it sprung back to life as if it had never seen death. She closed her eyes again; once they were open they were a pale color, and the air in the bar begin to whip to and fro with a fury, pushing the husky woman back a few paces.

"I think I'm good, Merdna. I have control over the elements, I don't need any more training," She said haughtily, finally turning to look at the old woman.

Merdna furrowed her brow even lower to an almost unibrow state, "Young Lady," she aggressively tried to hide her irritation, "if you were to become Mother Nature in your current state the scales would certainly tip in the other direction!"

Ini'el slapped the bar and stood to her feet, "Screw the scales! Let them tip!"

She got up from the barstool in a huff and made to storm out of the tavern, but the husky woman stood in her way.

"This is not my birthright," growled Ini'el as the two women glared at each other for a long moment.

"No, but it is your destiny. Your sister is gone, and her burden has become yours. If a new Mother is not named soon the balance between chaos and order will tip, and it *is* your birthright to keep that from happening."

She placed a reassuring hand on Ini'el's shoulder, "It is good that you have control over the elements, but you have not yet mastered creation or unity. Without all three skills you are vulnerable to chaos."

Ini'el shrugged her off and exited the tavern without another word. She stood outside of the doorway and let the heat from the three suns wash over her. Her wavy hair blew in the slight breeze as she began her walk back to Veros. She could see the red leaves from the great tree colored against the desert landscape, and a small frown found her lips.

She loved Veros, the city carved into a giant red-maple tree, the heart of the land of Neither. However, she did not want to spend the rest of her life there. Since an early age she had always dreamed of running away to The Surface, the realm of mankind, but her dreams were washed away the day her twin sister disappeared. Ini'el was now the heir to the throne to become the next Mother Nature, Goddess of Order, a title she despised. If only she could find her sister this whole nightmare would be over, but all entry and exit from Neither was sealed after Gem'el disappeared.

"INI'EL!" a voice from her past whispered on the wind as a memory resurfaced. "INI'EL!" she was a kid again. It was fourteen years ago. She was dashing through the Whistling Woods, named after the leaves that sounded like a thousand birds chirping when the wind would blow by. She was barefoot as she ran through the brush chasing after a Fury while her sister trailed behind her begging her to stop. She felt the cold of the earth on the bottoms of her feet, and her laughter rang out loud mixing with the chirp of the leaves to form a harmonious tune.

They were deep within the woods, further than they had ever been before, but Ini'el was not afraid. Her sister was with her and she was strong; if any of the creatures of the forest tried anything Gem'el would surely take them down. She continued to chase the three-tailed, foxlike Fury as it bounded through the woods. On and on they went until it disappeared.

"Where'd it…" The girls stopped as a thick grey fog settled all around them.

"Ini'el we need to go now," Gem'el grabbed her sisters' hand and tried to pull her, but Ini'el snatched her hand away.

"No, I want the Fury. I'm not leaving without him!"

"It's not safe. We'll come back for it, but we have to go now," she pleaded.

She tried to persuade her sister to leave the clearing, but Ini'el was stubborn, and, unfortunately, the moment to flee had already faded. The fog had become dense and obstructed the view of their escape. Gem'el could not tell which way was forward or which way was back. They were trapped.

"Get behind me," Gem'el knew they could not run; the only other option was to fight. She held Ini'el behind her and readied herself.

The fog began to stir and shift when a hand reached out for the girls. Gem'el's eyes became a brilliant white light, and she pushed a gust of wind with her palm making the approaching hand disappear. Shrill laughs erupted from all around them.

"The girl is an elemental!" came a screech of a voice. The laughter erupted again.

The voices started whispering and whirling all around them, when suddenly, as if by some miracle an opening formed. Without hesitation Gem'el took her sister's hand, and they leapt through it to dash through the woods. Gem'el saw the fog break apart into several separate smoke-like beings, their glowing purple eyes looking after the girls.

"What are those things?" Ini'el cried.

"Smov. They're creatures of fog; spirits. They're humans corrupted by magic."

They ran as fast as they could, but no matter how far they went they could feel the Smov all around them, chasing them, watching their every move. One swooped in front of them in a cloud of fog before taking shape; its gaseous hair flowed and rippled; its glowing eyes stared down at them, and the outline of its face and torso dripped into a smoke like tail. Ini'el could only take in its presence for a moment before her sister yanked her away. The Smov continued chasing them and cutting them off, leading them deeper into the woods.

Ini'el prayed for release from the horrid nightmare, and as if her prayers had been answered, Gem'el cried out in victory having spotted a break in the trees. They had made it to the forest's edge. They were free. The girls rejoiced, and the scenery seemed to bleed together as they picked up momentum. The forest spat them out into a small clearing, and they collapsed in joy on the outskirts of the trees thinking they had outrun their predators.

Their relief was short-lived, however, the group of Smov came bustling through the trees like a thick cloud of terror. Ini'el screamed while the whispers grew louder and louder with the Smov swimming around them clawing at the air.

"The girl screams!" a voice cackled. "Hopefully, they won't figure out our weakness of earth from an elemental's touch!" The laughing grew louder and louder.

"Gem'el!"

"I know! Get behind me!" Gem'el's eyes grew to a blinding green light; she lifted her hands and vines from the earth reached up and impaled the group of Smov. The laughing grew even louder. The Smov separated momentarily before getting back into formation, and Ini'el closed her eyes and covered her ears when the sound became unbearable.

"Such a jokester that one is! Everyone knows our weakness is wind from an elemental's touch!" one of the Smov laughed while they took position across from the girls.

Gem'el's eyes grew brilliant white. She pushed her hands together forming a ball of wind in the center before slowly releasing her hands causing the ball to grow larger and larger as she went. Once she was pleased with the size she pushed it with all her might into the Smov.

Once again, the Smov dissipated, but only for a moment. The laughs came back stronger and shriller than ever, "No, no! Wind doesn't hurt us! Water! Water is our downfall!"

The Smov positioned themselves behind the girls, and Gem'el wiped a bead of sweat from her forehead. Using her powers back to back like that was a bit exhausting, but she powered through. Her eyes began to glow blue and water sprang up from the cracks of the earth. She moved it gently through the air then whipped it towards the Smov.

The Smov laughed even louder and didn't even bother pretending to fade away before moving to another spot.

"FIRE, GIRL, FIRE!!!" The voice was crazed and exuberant and it echoed through the air.

"Gem, no." Ini'el grabbed her sister's hand softly while looking around the fog. She inspected the previous spots the creatures had been and noticed faint glowing symbols on gravestone like structures through the thick layer of Smov. They were ancient Verosian symbols for earth, water, and wind; She could not help but feel like something wasn't right.

"I think that's what they want. It's not going to hurt them, Gem. Don't do it. This is what they want."

Ini'el pleaded with her sister, but there was a rage burning inside of Gem'el that no number of cries could vanquish. Her eyes glowed an igneous orange, and the palms of her hands began to pulse. Flames sparked from her fingertips, and she brought them to her face and inspected them in wonderment. She had never created an element before. Usually the element had to be around, and she would just manipulate it, but this flame was internal. She could feel it, like the flames in her hand were just an extension of herself.

"GIRL!" one of the Smov hissed.

Gem'el snapped out of her thoughts and remembered what she was doing. She extended her hands forward, and the flames ripped through the air and found the Smov. Their laughs bounced all around them. The cloud dispersed and the Smov began to whirl and dance around.

"Yes! Yeeeeeessssss! Master shall return!"

One of the Smov took shape in front of the girls and stroked Gem'el's cheek. "Thank-you, Girl."

The Smov turned back into a cloud of smoke and drifted back into the air to join the rest as the ground began to shake.

Ini'el dug her claws into Gem'el's arm, and the sisters trembled while the earth underneath them continued to quake. Ini'el noticed a final gravestone which was hidden previously by the Smov. It held the symbol for fire and was now glowing like the rest. The earth stone began to sink into the ground, followed by the wind and water stones. The fire stone grew brighter, and the air around it seemed to take on the light.

The light began to sway, and the gravestone seemed to melt into it then reform into a different shape. It made a circle in the air, but behind it was not the land of Neither. Inside the circle there was only darkness. Ini'el investigated the darkness and heard a shrill scream which caused an icy chill to run up her spine. She felt a dark presence enter her mind, her eyes rolled into the back of her head, and her body went limp.

She woke up to a scratchy sensation, and when her eyes focused she noticed the tiny Fury from before licking her cheek. For a moment she was happy, but then she remembered what had just transpired. She leaned into a sitting position and looked around for her sister. There was no sign of her and the portal to the darkness was gone as well. Her heart started beating fast with a panic, and she jumped to her feet, "Gem'el!"

She screamed and ran around in a circle unsure if she should leave or stay where she was.

"Gem'el!" Tears started to swell in her eyes as she feared the worst. "Gem'el!" she cried out. The Fury started barking and Ini'el turned towards it. Its overly large ears were pulled back and its black beady eyes were pointed towards the sky. Ini'el looked up and her eyes widened in horror at what she saw.

A man with several scars across his face and one arm made of wood was holding an unconscious Gem'el in his arms as they ascended further into the sky. A portal was open above them, and Ini'el could not see anything but blue and what looked like clouds. She began running towards her sister knowing she could never reach the sky. She screamed her name as she went, tears falling all around her and the Fury keeping pace. She ran as far as she could, but the man and her sister were eventually enveloped by the portal, and it closed behind them without a trace. She fell to her knees in defeat and collapsed under the exhaustion of it all.

Ini'el sighed as the memory faded, and she looked up into the pink sky. She knew her sister was up there somewhere, somewhere on The Surface. If only she could get to her and bring her back, then this whole "becoming Mother" ordeal would be behind her. Her sister would be Mother Nature, and Ini'el would be free to live her life as she saw fit. No responsibility, no destiny, just being.

"Hey! Look out! Hey!"

She turned and noticed a large beast barreling towards her. Its top fangs were overgrown, protruding outside of its mouth, its ears seemed too big for its body, and its small eyes were black all the way around. It darted straight for Ini'el and was soon upon her, its frame hulking over her own, but she did not flinch.

"Look out!"

She noticed a boy running after the beast. He was wearing strange boots and wore a deep red cloak, and he was waving a stick wildly in the air with a panicked look etched into his face. The beast lunged at her with its enormous jaws open wide and still she did not move. It came to a halt right in front of her, stuck it's tongue out, and sloppily licked her face.

The boy came to a halt behind it as Ini'el began to pet the beast, "What in the world?" He looked on in bewilderment.

Ini'el stifled a giggle, "This is Oen, he wouldn't hurt a fly." Oen slammed his three tails into the ground causing loud thuds as they wagged back and forth.

"I find that hard to believe."

She noticed the stick in his hand was more intricate than she had perceived. He held it by a knob at the end and wooden vines seemed to stretch from the knob all the way to the point.

"What is that?" she inquired.

The boy noticed what she was staring at, and he quickly shoved it into his long boots and covered his boot with his cloak.

"Nothing," he said unconvincingly.

"Em." At her command Oen ceased being playful and turned towards the boy. Oen bared his teeth, and the hair on his back stood up and began to smoke. The air surrounding them grew hot and sticky, and flames began to drip from Oen's mouth.

"Did you want to lie to me again?"

The boy hesitantly reached down to his boot and re-retrieved the object without breaking eye-contact with the Fury. He handed it to her and she accepted it with a smile. It felt warm to the touch like something was alive inside. She sniffed it and held it next to her ear trying to learn its secrets, for it was clearly no ordinary stick. She shook it vigorously, and the boy reached out in a panic but quickly retracted when Oen growled sinisterly.

"Be careful with that, will ya!" He spoke to Ini'el, but his eyes never moved from Oen, "and can you call off your attack dog!?"

"What is this?" She asked without acknowledging his concerns.

"What does it look like?" He responded shortly.

She raised an eyebrow towards him, "Oen..."

He shot his hands up in defense, "It's a wand, it's a wand!"

"A w... A WAND!? You're a magician, a human?"

"Yes," he said in a tone that suggested it was none of her business.

"How did you get here?" She looked from the boy back to the wand with incredulous wonder.

He looked like he did not want to answer, but after a grimace from Oen, the boy was biddable, "I used a Genesis Coin."

Her eyes widened with glee, "I thought they were all destroyed!"

"Most were," he admitted.

"You can take me to The Surface!" It was more of a statement than a question.

"No," He responded. His tone was absolute.

"What? Why not?"

"Because, I don't go up there. Magicians are being hunted, and I'd rather stay here and not be slaughtered."

She scoffed, "Oh, so you're a coward."

"Through and through. Now, can you give me my wand back? I sort of need it."

She pondered for a moment. "Only if you agree to take me to The Surface." She said slyly.

He stared at her, then at the beast, and knowing he was out of options he agreed to her request. "Fine."

She smiled from ear to ear and handed him his wand back, but her happiness was short lived when a devious smile stretched across his face. "Thanks."

He whipped the wand in a patterned motion, "Rapipdeas," the word hung in the air and the magician started to fade leaving behind his smile like the Cheshire Cat; a moment later the smile vanished too.

"No!" Ini'el looked all around but the magician was nowhere to be found. "Oen can you track him?"

Oen sniffed the ground where the magician once stood. He caught the magician's scent and howled at the sky. "Good, let's hunt us a magician."

She had finally found a way to The Surface, and there was no way she was letting it go that easily. There was still a chance she could get her sister back, and she would not have to become Mother Nature in her place. Oen took off running and Ini'el followed close behind.

Once they were gone there was a whisper on the wind, and, standing in the same spot as if he had never left, the magician reappeared. He smiled cunningly after the girl and her beast and walked away in the opposite direction.

Syndicate 6ix Part Two:

Order and Chaos

Available now!

A Note From the Author:
Eric Raymond

I hope you enjoy the story and continue to follow along Declan's journey. He will return in <u>Syndicate 6ix: Blue Moon</u>

Please leave a review wherever you picked this book up, and if you would like to connect with me you can contact me at ericraymondbooks.com or on social media.

Until next time,

Eric R.

Instagram: @ericraymondbooks

Twitter: @eraymondbooks

Made in the USA
Coppell, TX
28 December 2019

13824082R00044